Gopher Takes Heart

VIRGINIA SCRIBNER
illustrated by JANET WILSON

VIKING

VIKING
Published by the Penguin Group
Penguin Books USA Inc., 375 Hudson Street, New York,
New York 10014, U.S.A.
Penguin Books Ltd, 27 Wrights Lane, London W8 5TZ, England
Penguin Books Australia Ltd, Ringwood, Victoria, Australia
Penguin Books Canada Ltd, 10 Alcorn Avenue,
Toronto, Ontario, Canada, M4V 3B2
Penguin Books (N.Z.) Ltd, 182–190 Wairau Road, Auckland 10, New Zealand

Penguin Books Ltd, Registered Offices: Harmondsworth, Middlesex, England

First published in 1993 by Viking, a division of Penguin Books USA Inc.

1   3   5   7   9   10   8   6   4   2

LIBRARY OF CONGRESS CATALOGING-IN-PUBLICATION DATA
Scribner, Virginia.
Gopher takes heart / by Virginia Scribner; illustrated by Janet Wilson
p.   cm.
Summary: While the fifth grade prepares for Valentine's Day,
Gopher struggles to stand up to the class bully, hold on to his milk
money, and retain his self-respect.
ISBN 0-670-84839-5
[1. Bullies—Fiction.   2. Schools—Fiction.   3.Valentine's Day—Fiction.
4. Self-esteem—Fiction]   I. Wilson, Janet, 1962– ill.   II. Title.
PZ7.S43615Go   1993   [Fic]—dc20   92-25939   CIP   AC

To my mother, Pauline Smith Scribner,
and my departed mother-in-law,
Wadia Deeb Abushanab

I would like to thank my editor,
Elizabeth Law, and
Mrs. Lori Rathbone and her fifth graders
at Chariho Middle School.
—V.S.

Many thanks to Mrs. Olszewski,
Johnny Stacey, and their class at
Terry Fox Public School.
—J.W.

Contents

A Couple of Dimes

Gopher reached for the brown leather purse on top of the refrigerator. "I'm taking the two dimes, okay?" he called. He had to speak loudly to get above the roar of his mother's hair dryer.

"Okay," she called back.

Gopher found the two dimes and put the purse back. Now, let's see. He had his lunch, his milk money, his homework. He grabbed an apple from the counter. He'd eat that on the way. He guessed he was ready to leave for school.

"Bye, Mom. Bye, Dad," he called, halfway out the door.

"What?" His mother abruptly turned off the

hair dryer. "What time is it, anyhow? I'm going to be late for work!"

"No, you've got time. I'm leaving fifteen minutes early. Bye."

Gopher quickly closed the door. As good as his parents were about understanding things, he didn't want to tell them why he was leaving early.

He took a bite of apple and started the eight-block walk to school. Unfortunately, it was only seven blocks to Fletcher Simpson's house. Fletcher was in Gopher's fifth-grade class at Lincoln Elementary School. For the last month, every time Gopher walked past that yellow house with green shutters, Fletcher would be waiting for him. He'd stand next to a sign that said SLOW—CHILDREN, hold out his big grubby hand, and say in a singsongy way, "Hand it over."

"It" was Gopher's milk money.

Today as Gopher approached the house he didn't see Fletcher standing in his usual spot. Maybe his plan was working. Today he'd finally be able to buy a milk. Stephanie wouldn't be able to tease him, "What's the matter, you got eggplant for brains?"

Then he heard a sickening noise. "Hey, Gopher, wait up." It was Fletcher. He was bounding toward him like a huge, slavering dog. He wasn't wearing a jacket, even though it was February, still pretty cold.

Gopher considered what to do. If he ran, Fletcher would catch up with him. Then he'd be nastier than usual. Gopher had tried it a couple of times. One time Fletcher had stolen his homework as well as his milk money. Another time he had grabbed a handful of dirt and shaken it over Gopher's head. Gopher decided to stop.

In a second Fletcher was standing directly in front of him, his arms folded across his chest. "So, you thought you'd sneak by me this morning, huh?" As usual, he was speaking in that terrible singsongy voice.

"I wasn't sneaking," Gopher answered.

"How come you're so early today, Gopher

Grub? You made me come out in the middle of my breakfast. That makes me *angry*."

"You mean you got up in the middle of your breakfast just to steal my lousy milk money?" Gopher put all the disgust he could into his voice.

"Your money's not lousy . . . not like the rest of you." Fletcher was shivering. "Hurry up, I'm cold."

Gopher decided to try something daring. "I don't have any milk money today," he said.

Fletcher hesitated, but only for a second. "You're lying."

"No, I'm not. You keep stealing it. I'd have to be pretty stupid to keep bringing it."

Fletcher eyed him suspiciously. "Well, if you don't have any money, why are you so early this morning?" He yanked Gopher by the collar. "Huh?"

As usual, Fletcher had Gopher so rattled he couldn't think. Why was he so early? "I, er, I . . . wanted to talk to Mrs. Morrison about some math problems."

But his stammering had given him away. "You're a lousy liar," jeered Fletcher. "Give me the money or your head will look like a deflated basketball. And hurry up, I'm freezing."

Something about seeing Fletcher Simpson shivering in the cold made Gopher feel good. He decided to keep it going. "How can I give you something I don't have?" he asked.

Fletcher pounced at him and grabbed him around the neck with both hands. "Stop stalling and give it to me."

"Let go of my neck," Gopher gasped. He wriggled free. "If you keep this up, you'll go to jail just like your brother."

"I hope I *do* go to jail. My brother says all you do is watch television and play volleyball. It sounds better than going to stupid school."

"Sure," said Gopher.

Fletcher came close again. "C'mon, hand it over. I want to go back in the house."

Gopher decided to try something else. He'd just pretend Fletcher wasn't there. He started walking past him. Fletcher grabbed him by the shoulder.

"Hey, what do you think you're doing?" Fletcher was clearly getting angrier and angrier. He punched Gopher a hard one right in the chest.

Gopher knew he'd lost. Pretty soon Fletcher might really start beating him up. What were a couple of dimes anyway? He took the dimes out of his pocket, flung them at Fletcher's feet, and darted past. "Here, take 'em!"

Fletcher jumped to avoid being hit by the money. "Hey, squirt, don't you do that again!"

Again. Again. Again. The word thumped in Gopher's mind like a flat tire on his bike. As he hurried on to school he wondered, Was that slimeball Fletcher going to keep this up forever?

All Because of
the Contest

Gopher turned to see if Fletcher was following him. He wasn't. He had picked up the money and was walking back to his house.

Gopher slowed down. He didn't want to arrive at school before he had a chance to calm down. He bit his lip and blinked back the hot wetness in his eyes. His throat felt as if someone had poured warm glue down it.

Fletcher probably *will* end up in jail like his brother, he thought. Gopher knew all about it. For weeks Fletcher had gone around bragging how his brother had been in a bar one night, gotten into a fight, and stabbed a guy in the stomach. You'd think in a small town like this, the story would have made the front page of the paper. But it hadn't. The only way Gopher knew about it was from Fletcher.

Gopher wondered how a guy who went around stabbing people could be good in art. That was something he *had* read about in the paper. Right on the front page it had said, "Foster Simpson Elected Senior Class Artist." It had explained that every year the graduating high school seniors voted on projects submitted by their fellow classmates. At first Gopher couldn't believe that Foster Simpson was really Fletcher's brother, the same one who was in jail. But the address the paper had given was the same as Fletcher's, so Gopher figured it had to be.

After reading the article, Gopher hoped someday *he* might win the prize. That's why he'd made a special trip over to the high school to see Fletcher's brother's project.

Fletcher's brother had called his project "Caveman's Computer." It was really funny and clever. No wonder it had been voted the best.

Not like Fletcher's project in Ms. Connors's Christmas contest, Gopher thought. In fact, that contest was the reason Fletcher had started stealing Gopher's milk money in the first place.

Ms. Connors had had all the kids in Special Art Class make something "Christmasy or wintery." Gopher had painted a picture of Santa brushing down Rudolph. Fletcher had made a caveman's Christmas tree. It was really something. It was about two feet high, molded out of clay. He had painted it green and glued on all different kinds of caveman ornaments, like dried-out meat bones that looked like dinosaur bones and some fur cut into shapes like stretched-out animal skins. And then to make it really funny he had stuck on lots of shiny beads with plastic string running between them to look like electric lights. Like sure, cavemen had a place to plug in lights!

Gopher secretly liked Fletcher's tree a lot more than his own oil painting of Santa brushing down Rudolph, but he hadn't voted for it.

He wasn't going to vote for *anything* Fletcher made. A lot of other kids must have felt the same way. Fletcher had gotten only four votes. Gopher had gotten over a hundred.

But Fletcher's stealing his milk money every morning had gotten so bad since then that Gopher almost wished he hadn't won. He wished at least that the principal, Mr. Swenson, would take down the Santa picture from the bulletin board outside his office. Then maybe Fletcher would start to forget about the contest. Anyway, it looked a little silly having a picture of Santa up now that it was the middle of February. It was two days before Valentine's Day, for Pete's sake!

Gopher looked back at the yellow house with green shutters to see if Fletcher was coming. He wasn't. "That needle-neck!" he said to himself. As he started walking again he remembered Fletcher had said he'd been eating breakfast. Gopher could imagine him inside his house, stuffing his face with some soggy cereal covered with mushy banana slices. Then

Gopher suddenly got an image of himself taking a big rotten banana and mashing it right in Fletcher's face.

No, that wouldn't work. Fletcher would just beat him up real bad and probably mash the banana right back in *his* face.

Gopher changed the picture. This time Fletcher was in jail. He was standing glumly behind iron bars and the cell was painted that pukey jail yellow, like the ones Gopher had seen at Alcatraz last summer. And Fletcher was wearing one of those black-and-white suits, like prisoners used to wear.

"Serves you right for tormenting me all those years," Gopher would say, continuing the movie in his head.

Fletcher would make a wild lunge at him. He'd put his arms through the bars and growl, but Gopher would be standing just far enough away so he couldn't reach him. "Ha, ha!" he would laugh meanly. "When are you going to pay me back all the milk money you took, you big fat cheapo?"

Then Fletcher would start to howl, he'd be so mad! And Gopher would dig in his pocket for his rotten banana and he'd smash it into Fletcher's face, right in the eyes.

"Hey, guard!" Fletcher would wail, rubbing away at sticky, oozing banana. Gopher would hear the guard's footsteps and start to make his frantic getaway.

———

Gopher was so caught up in his daydream that as he looked around he almost expected to see a prison guard chasing him.

Of course, there wasn't any. There was just the usual morning scene of kids milling around the schoolyard, waiting for the bell to ring.

And Fletcher wasn't in jail. He'd be arriving at school any minute now. Gopher's throat started filling with glue again. Another day of being pushed around by Fletcher.

Planning the Party

"Hey, Gopher, c'mere."

It was Stephanie. She was standing among a small group of their classmates.

Gopher wasn't surprised Stephanie was the one who noticed him. She was always doing stuff like that. She had curly black hair, a cute nose, and the most beautiful smile you could imagine. And she wore braces! Gopher could never figure out how a girl who had all those little metal things all over her mouth could have such a nice smile, but Stephanie sure did. He liked her the most of any girl in Mrs. Morrison's class.

Gopher walked over to the group. "We're planning a surprise Valentine's Day party for Friday," Stephanie whispered. "Wanna help?"

Gopher felt like he'd just won the grand prize in some kind of contest. Here were his best friends in Mrs. Morrison's class asking *him* to help. They didn't think he was a creep. They thought he was an okay guy.

"We thought we'd have every kid bring in a quarter tomorrow," said Brenda, who, as always, had put herself in charge. "Kevin, you figure it out. You're good in math."

Kevin, doing as he was told, got out a piece of paper and a pencil. "Now, if we get twenty-five cents from each kid, and there are twenty-five kids in the class . . . hmm, let's see." He proceeded to multiply. "That would be six dollars and twenty-five cents."

"Yeah, but you're forgetting that Fletcher won't bring in a quarter," said Lance. "Remember how he didn't give any money toward Mrs. Morrison's Christmas present?"

Everyone agreed it was very unlikely that Fletcher would bring in a quarter. They would count on having only six dollars for the Valentine's Day party.

"Well, I think we should at least ask him," said Stephanie. "Maybe he's changed since Christmas."

Gopher felt like saying that he was sure Fletcher had *not* changed, at least as of a few minutes ago. But he didn't want to give away what had happened on the way to school.

Brenda and the rest of the group continued to plan the party. "We will have three dollars to buy food and three dollars to buy a real fancy valentine for Mrs. Morrison." That was okay with everyone. "Robin, you buy the food," Brenda ordered. Then she turned to Gopher. "Since you're the best one in art, would you pick out the valentine?"

Would he? He'd be proud to! Being asked to pick out the most important part of the party almost made up for having to live in the same world with Fletcher Simpson.

Then he had an even better idea. Maybe he could *make* the valentine. With three dollars he could buy a big piece of red velvet and cover it with lace and ribbons and fake jewels and all that kind of stuff. He told the others his plan.

"What a great idea!" said Kevin. "Make it really big. The biggest in the world. Maybe we could get it into *The Guinness Book of World Records*."

"I can just see Mrs. Morrison's face," said Robin. "She'll faint!"

"You know what else is great about Gopher's idea?" asked Lance. "We'll all have room to sign our names really big. I can just see it now—this tremendous valentine, as big as the whole blackboard."

"Let's make sure we've got this straight," said Brenda. "The kids bring in their quarters tomorrow. Robin and Gopher buy the stuff after school. Then the next day, which is Friday, they bring their stuff in, and we have the party that afternoon. Great!"

The first bell rang. It was time to go into the building. "Have we forgotten anything?" asked Brenda.

"Just one thing," said Robin. "Who's going to collect the money?"

Brenda gave her a what-a-stupid-question look. *Who* did she think?

"But we forgot something else," added Lance. "How are we going to tell everyone to bring in a quarter without Mrs. Morrison finding out?"

"That's no problem," said Brenda. "Everyone tell all the kids in your row. None of us sits in row four, so I'll tell them."

"Even Fletcher?" someone teased.

"Sure, why not?" Brenda held up a clenched fist. "And if he gives me any trouble, he gets one of these."

Everyone laughed. They knew Brenda was just showing off. She wouldn't really beat up Fletcher.

But if it was up to Gopher, he'd sure like to see her try!

Gopher's
"Big Brother"

Gopher didn't feel like walking to school the next morning. He knew Fletcher would take his milk money *and* his party money if he had the chance. Gopher sure didn't want to be the only one not to pay a quarter. The only one besides Fletcher, that is.

He thought about how he could get out of walking to school. The only idea that came to him was asking his father for a ride. Luckily, his father said yes without asking too many questions.

From the car Gopher saw Fletcher waiting beside the SLOW—CHILDREN sign. He slid down in his seat so Fletcher wouldn't see him.

"What are you doing, Matt?" his father asked. Gopher's father, like all grown-ups, refused to call him anything but Matt or Matthew, his real first name. "Gopher" came from kids putting an *-er* onto his last name, Goff.

"Just kind of lounging here, Dad," Gopher answered.

"Hmmm," his father said with a puzzled expression. "What time did you go to bed last night?"

Gopher assured his father he was all right and stuck his head up just enough to see if Fletcher had recognized the car. Rats! He had! As soon as their car drove by, Fletcher started running toward the school.

Gopher jumped out almost before the car had stopped moving. "Bye, Dad, thanks." Now, if he could just put away his jacket on his hook in the hallway and get into class. He wasn't really safe from Fletcher until he was *in* the classroom.

Having reached the hallway, he gave his jacket zipper a quick, hard jerk. "Oh, no!" he muttered. He had jammed the zipper.

"Did Gopher Grub get a ride from his daddy this morning?" called Fletcher as he walked up to his coathook, the one right next to Gopher's. "I saw your car. I also know *why* you wanted a ride."

"Leave me alone," muttered Gopher. He was holding his lunch bag and his math book in one hand. With the other he was struggling with the stuck zipper.

"I heard about bringing in a quarter," Fletcher went on. "You didn't want me to take your precious quarter for your precious valentine party, did you?"

Fletcher's jacket was now off, and he was ready to go into the classroom. He looked more closely at what Gopher was doing. "Is little Gopher having trouble with his little zipper?"

Gopher didn't answer. He hoped Fletcher would just leave. He dropped his math book on the floor and held his lunch bag with his teeth. Now he could tackle the zipper with both hands. By this time all the other kids were in class.

"What's this?" said Fletcher, turning his attention to Gopher's math book. He poked at it with his toe.

"Leaf my book awone," Gopher mumbled through the lunch bag. He continued struggling with the zipper. Fletcher gave the book a good kick. "Leaf id awone, I said."

Fletcher walked over to the book, picked it up, and started paging through it. "Oh, looky here." He plucked Gopher's math homework from the book. "This paper might be worth forty-five cents." So! Fletcher *did* want the party money as well as the milk money.

At last Gopher had the jacket off and the lunch bag out from between his teeth. He grabbed for the paper. "Give it back," he ordered. Fletcher held it beyond his outstretched hand.

"I'll give it back for forty-five cents."

Gopher knew Fletcher wouldn't take a chance on beating him up right here in the school building. He shook his head. "No way!"

"No way? No way, you say?" Fletcher

waved the homework in front of Gopher's face. "O-kay." On the "okay" he ripped the paper in two. He stuffed the ripped paper back into the book, threw the book on the floor, and walked toward the classroom. "See ya, squirt."

Gopher went over to pick up the book. He hated that Fletcher! Hated him! He wished so much that someone would take a big knife and stab him in the stomach. Just like his brother had done to that other guy.

"I'm going to have my big brother beat you up when he gets home from the army," Gopher blurted out.

"I didn't know you had a big brother," Fletcher said, not even turning around. "If he's anything like you, he's not much to worry about."

"Yeah? Well, he could handle *you* easy enough." Gopher watched Fletcher walk away and enter the classroom. He was glad he had threatened Fletcher with something—even if it wasn't true. How he wished he really did have a big brother! How he wished that big brother was there right then! *He* could beat up Fletcher. When he was done, Fletcher would look like a hot dog with lots of ketchup and mustard on it that had been stepped on by about five hundred dirty shoes. That would be just what Fletcher deserved!

Gopher picked up the math book and went into the classroom. Would he *ever* think of a way to really get Fletcher?

Announcements

As Gopher entered the classroom, he saw Brenda buzzing around collecting quarters. When she stopped at Fletcher's desk, he didn't give her one. She just moved on to the next person. After she had all the quarters, she quietly left the room.

Mrs. Morrison had been so absorbed in talking to a couple of boys at her desk that she apparently hadn't noticed what was going on. "My, everybody's keyed up today," she declared when she finally looked up. "It's not because tomorrow's Valentine's Day, is it, by any chance?" Everybody giggled. Mrs. Morrison smiled.

The class got down to work. After a few

minutes the loudspeaker squawked, "Mrs. Morrison, you have a call in the office."

"Class, just continue what you're doing. I'll be right back," she said.

As soon as Mrs. Morrison was safely out of the room, Brenda scrambled in. She looked pleased with herself. "Quiet! Quiet!" she shouted. When the class was looking at her, she began. "I told Mrs. Lacey in the office to stall her as long as possible. But we don't have much time." She glowered at two girls in the back who weren't paying attention.

"As you all know, we've planned a surprise party for tomorrow for Mrs. Morrison. We have exactly six dollars to spend, since everyone brought in a quarter today." She tilted her head in Fletcher's direction. *"Except one person."* Gopher enjoyed the way the kids glared at Fletcher when Brenda said that last part.

"I just went to the office and changed the quarters into dollars." Brenda reached into her pocket and brought out a handful of dollar bills.

"I'm giving these three dollars to Robin. She's going to buy the food." Brenda slowly counted out three dollars and handed them to Robin.

"And I'm giving these three dollars to Gopher. He's going to buy the valentine." She walked over to Gopher's desk and repeated the performance of counting out the money.

Gopher expected her to sit down at this point. He wasn't sure why she had to make an announcement out of handing out the money anyway. Everyone already knew about the party. They'd all brought in their quarters, hadn't they?

"At first," Brenda continued, "we were going to have Gopher get a regular store-bought valentine. You know, one of those fancy ones that cost about three dollars." She made a face: who'd want a valentine like that? "But then he had this terrific idea to *make* the valentine. He said he could make a much bigger and fancier one."

Brenda glanced over at Lance, who was

watching for Mrs. Morrison's return. "No sign of her yet," he called.

Brenda went on. "Yes, Gopher's going to make us a *tremendous* valentine out of velvet and lace and ribbons and stuff like that."

Gopher heard quiet *oohs* and *ahhs* from various parts of the room. Everyone was obviously impressed with the big job he had ahead of him. He smiled an embarrassed smile.

"And besides that . . . " Brenda talked on. Gopher felt the tops of his ears turning warm. Wouldn't that blabbermouth Brenda *ever* sit down? By now, all the kids must be expecting something as big and fancy as those Rose Bowl floats they show on TV every New Year's Day.

"Sit down, Brenda," hissed Lance. "Here she comes." Everyone ducked back to work.

"I trust you've all been working hard while I was gone?" asked Mrs. Morrison as she walked in.

When the class went to morning recess, Gopher was still a little dizzy. All that attention. All those kids expecting something "tremendous." He sure hoped he wouldn't disappoint them.

But why should he? He was good in art. He had won the Christmas art contest, hadn't he? He *could* do it! He remembered what his mother always said when he complained he couldn't do something: "Take heart and take action." She thought that believing you could do something was half of actually doing it. Gopher didn't know if it was *half*—maybe a quarter. Anyway, he'd do it!

He began to feel a little glad Brenda had made such a big deal out of the valentine. It *was* a big deal. He'd make his classmates the best valentine . . . they'd all be so proud of him . . .

"Hey, Gopher, c'mon. We're starting a baseball game," Kevin called.

"Nah, I don't feel like it." Gopher wanted to be alone for a while. He wanted to walk around and think. How could he design a really great valentine, one the kids would talk about for months and months? As he walked he felt like he was being carried away into the cool blue February sky by a giant rainbow-colored hot-air balloon.

Squish. Without realizing it, he had walked to the end of the playground and stepped into a soggy snow pile. He turned to walk back.

Pop! The rainbow-colored hot-air balloon burst. There was Fletcher, standing five feet away.

From Pocket to Pocket

"So, the biggest little squirt in Rhode Island is going to make the class valentine?" jeered Fletcher, using that terrible singsongy voice. "Isn't that cute." He walked closer. "Is it going to be a *big* valentine, and are all the little kiddies going to sign their names?"

Gopher looked to see who was around. Nobody! Where had he ever gotten this brilliant idea of walking alone?

"You don't have to sign it," he said. He felt like adding that Fletcher didn't have the *right* to sign it, since he hadn't brought in a quarter, but he decided he'd better not.

"Don't worry, dumbface," said Fletcher, "I wouldn't be caught dead signing any valentine *you* made."

Gopher hated the insulting tone of Fletcher's voice, but as always, he felt helpless to do anything about it. He started to walk away.

Fletcher followed. Every time Gopher turned to walk back to the building, Fletcher blocked his path. In a few minutes Fletcher had steered him around the corner of the building. Now they were out of sight of everybody else on the playground.

"I hope you have a good imagination, *Artie,*" said Fletcher. Gopher figured Fletcher thought that calling him Artie was a good way to make fun of his ability in art. Well, what about *him?* Fletcher liked art, too. In Special Art Ms. Connors had almost gone bonkers over his caveman Christmas tree.

Gopher tried to remain calm. Fletcher could do anything he wanted in this secluded part of the playground. "I have a couple of ideas," he answered quietly.

"That's good," replied Fletcher, "because you're going to need all the ideas you can get. You're going to have to make that so-called tremendous valentine out of newspaper and toilet paper and whatever else you happen to have around the house."

Now Gopher knew his worst fears were coming true. Fletcher was going to ask for the money! He decided to play dumb. "What do you mean by that? You know I'm going to buy all the stuff I need tonight after school." He *had* to get out of there! He was just about to make a dash for it when Fletcher caught his right arm.

"I *mean*, Artie," said Fletcher, squeezing the arm hard, "that I'm going to relieve you of those three dollars right now. I saw you put 'em in your pocket."

Gopher couldn't think of anything to say. Fletcher was about to steal the class money, and he, Gopher, was going to be the one to let him! He tried to free his arm, but Fletcher held on tight.

"I *said*, hand 'em over." By now Fletcher was bending Gopher's arm behind his back and pushing it toward his neck. It hurt like any-thing.

"Are you crazy or something?" shouted Gopher. He wondered if maybe *he* wasn't the one who was crazy. What was he doing here with Fletcher Simpson practically breaking his arm and the class's three dollars in his pocket? This *must* be a nightmare.

But the pain in his arm and shoulder con-vinced him that he wasn't dreaming. "It's bad enough that you pick on me and take my milk money," he stammered, "but to take the class money, that's t-too much."

"Just give me the moolah," whined Fletcher, sounding tired and annoyed. He gave Gopher's arm a jerk. Gopher felt as if his arm were being pulled out of its socket. Fletcher jerked again. "Give it to me!"

"Stop it! Stop it!" Gopher was begging now. "You're breaking my arm!"

Still Fletcher would not stop.

Gopher held out for a few more seconds. But

then, when he couldn't stand it anymore, "I'll . . . give you the . . . " He couldn't bring himself to finish the sentence.

Fletcher relaxed his hold a little. Gopher was gasping for breath. "I think . . . you . . . you . . . *stink!*" He reached into his pocket with his free hand. It was trembling so badly he could barely hand over the money. "Here!"

Fletcher grabbed the bills and let go of the arm. "I happen to have three dollars at home to replace it with," said Gopher. "Otherwise, you'd never get it out of me in a million years."

"That's a laugh," hooted Fletcher. "Getting money from you is as easy as taking candy from a baby. See ya. And I wouldn't tell anybody about this, if I were you."

Gopher watched helplessly as Fletcher put the money in his jacket pocket and walked away. "Just wait till my brother hears about this," he shouted at Fletcher's back. "You'll be sorry!"

Fletcher suddenly stopped and walked back,

putting his face close to Gopher's. "You don't catch on, do you, stupid?"

Gopher reeled. Now what was Fletcher going to do?

"I just said, don't tell anybody." Fletcher's face was pulled into a cartoonlike grimace. "That includes your brother. If you tell your brother, I'll tell my brother. And one of us— you, moron—won't *have* a brother after that."

With that he hunched his shoulders and walked away.

Stephanie Is Nice

Gopher could barely walk back to the school building. He felt sure everybody could tell what he'd been through just by looking at him. He wished he could find a corner someplace to go and die in.

The bell rang. Morning recess was over. When Gopher went to put his jacket on his coathook, Fletcher was there. "Remember what I said about—" Just then Stephanie walked up to Gopher, cutting Fletcher off.

"What's the matter, Gopher?" she asked in a worried voice. "You look like you were just run over by a truck." Gopher wasn't about to tell Stephanie, or anybody else, the real reason he looked so unhappy. He racked his brain for

another possible explanation. He remembered his torn-up math paper from that morning.

"Oh, I lost my math homework on the way to school," he mumbled, "and now I'll probably have to stay after. And I have so much to do to get the valentine ready by tomorrow. I know I'll never make it."

He glanced uneasily at Fletcher, who he knew was listening to every word.

"You're too much," said Stephanie with a light laugh. "You always do your work. Do you really believe Mrs. Morrison is going to keep you after school for *one* time?"

"Probably. With my luck." Gopher knew he looked ridiculous acting this unhappy about a lost math paper, but he couldn't help it. It was all he could do to keep from crying.

"Oh, Gopher!" Stephanie pretended she was annoyed with him, but there was a kindness in her voice. "I'll give you my homework to copy. It wouldn't be cheating since you did do the work. Then you won't have to worry about staying after. Okay?"

"Okay." Gopher managed a small grin.

"Will you three get into this classroom, please?" called Mrs. Morrison, who was waiting to close the door. Fletcher, Gopher, and Stephanie hurried into class.

In spite of himself, Gopher felt better. Stephanie really knew how to make a person feel good. How could people as nice as Stephanie be in the same world with people as rotten as Fletcher?

Fletcher! As Gopher remembered that stinking, stealing bully the sunshiny breeze of happiness he'd received from Stephanie turned into cloudy skies. Sure, she was nice to him; she was nice to everybody. But if she knew what a jerk he was, she probably wouldn't have anything to do with him.

Then a thought occurred to him that changed the cloudy skies into a thunderstorm. Brenda had given Robin three dollars, too. Why hadn't Fletcher taken *her* money? And Robin was a girl!

Gopher punched his hands in his pockets in

disgust. One fist hit the two dimes still there. "I guess the snake didn't think of those."

He glanced at Fletcher, who was gazing out the window. *And now he says he's going to have his brother beat up my brother*, he thought miserably. *What's he going to do when he finds out I don't even have one?*

There was a slight tap on his shoulder. Gopher turned around, and the boy behind him sneaked him a piece of lined yellow paper with writing on it. It was Stephanie's math homework! He had expected her to give it to him at lunchtime. Not now, during class! Mrs. Morrison got really mad when she caught kids copying each other's homework. Stephanie would take that chance? For *him?*

He looked over at her. "Thanks," he mouthed silently, putting all the gratitude he could into that one word.

She shrugged to say it was no big deal. Then she gave him a little wave—and one of those beautiful brace-y smiles.

A Filmstrip
on Gophers

"Class, today we're going to have a filmstrip about an animal that should be particularly interesting to at least one member of our class," Mrs. Morrison announced brightly as soon as everyone had taken their seats. "Can anyone guess what animal that would be?"

"*Gophers!*" called out several children at once.

"That's right." Mrs. Morrison smiled at Gopher. "Today we're going to learn what a *real* gopher looks like."

Gopher groaned. Usually he didn't mind being teased by grown-ups about his nickname. Today he definitely wasn't in the mood.

Gopher looked two rows over to see how Fletcher was reacting to what Mrs. Morrison had said. Their eyes met. Gopher turned away, but not before Fletcher had given him a goody-for-you fake smile.

"Stephanie," Mrs. Morrison called. "Would you please go to the library and ask if we might have the filmstrip on gophers? Mrs. Kelly knows the one I mean."

Stephanie, of course, agreed to go. "Now, while she's doing that, let's discuss what we already know about gophers."

Lance said that his uncle hated gophers because they dig underground tunnels in his lawn. Kevin said that was no reason to hate them, they had to live too, didn't they? Brenda told a long story about a gopher she saw on a trip to visit her aunt in Iowa last summer.

"I wonder what's keeping Stephanie?" said Mrs. Morrison, looking at the clock. "If she doesn't come soon, we won't be able to finish before lunch."

Just then Stephanie walked in carrying a small plastic canister in one hand and a cassette tape in the other.

"You were gone so long we thought you

went to Timbuktu," piped up Kevin.

Mrs. Morrison took the filmstrip and the cassette tape. Stephanie started to explain. "Mrs. Kelly said that Mr. Harris had it, and then I went to Mr. Harris, and he said he'd already returned it, so Mrs. Kelly looked some more, and then she finally found it."

"I see," said Mrs. Morrison. She was peering into the projector. The film seemed to be stuck.

"It had somehow gotten put in the wrong drawer," Stephanie continued. "Mrs. Kelly said she didn't have her glasses on when she put it away, and she thought the word *gophers* was *golfers,* so she put it in the sports drawer."

"In the *sports* drawer!" guffawed Kevin. "Boy, that's dumb!"

"Kevin," said Mrs. Morrison, looking like she was trying not to smile, "I don't think it's *your* job to comment on how dumb or smart Mrs. Kelly is. Now, would someone please turn off the lights?"

The projector hummed and a man's voice began. "Gophers are best known for their long underground tunnels." The guy said some other stuff about tunnels, and then he started talking about how gophers look. "Their most distinctive physical feature is usually considered to be their large fur-lined pouches, which open from the outside and extend to their shoulders."

"And you guys say *I* have a big mouth!" Kevin shouted from the darkness.

"Kevin, *pleeease*," said Mrs. Morrison.

The narrator went on to explain how gophers use these cheek pouches to carry food and nesting materials. Built-in pockets, thought Gopher idly. He wasn't really paying much attention, although this filmstrip was a little better than most.

Then it struck him. Pockets! Was there any chance that Fletcher had left the money in his jacket pocket?

The more Gopher thought about it, the more it seemed it had to be. Stephanie had been standing right there the whole time Fletcher was taking off his jacket. Afterward, Mrs. Morrison had called, and they'd all walked into class together. When would he have had a chance to take the money out of his pocket? It was probably too good to be true, but Gopher had to find out. He raised his hand.

"Yes, Matthew?"

"I don't feel well," he said. He guessed he didn't have to worry about being believed on that point. If he looked half, or even a quarter, as bad as he felt, anyone in the world could see he didn't feel well. "May I please go to the boys' room?"

"Couldn't you wait until the filmstrip is over? It's only a couple more minutes."

"No, ma'am. I really don't feel well." He held his stomach to indicate he might throw up.

"Well, then you'd better go. I know when you say something, it's the truth."

Gopher left the room and closed the door behind him. Mrs. Morrison's remark about his truthfulness made him feel a little guilty, but what could he do? This was an emergency.

She'd also said the filmstrip was almost over—he'd have to work fast.

Money in a Shoe

Gopher went to the coathooks and immediately found Fletcher's jacket. He put his hand into one of the pockets. No money there. It *has* to be here, he thought. It just *has* to. He put his hand into the other pocket. The delicious smoothness of three well-worn dollar bills met his fingers. He grabbed the money, stuffed it in his pocket, and ran to the boys' bathroom.

"Are you sick?" called out one of the secretaries as Gopher dashed past the office door. "No, I'm okay." Now was no time to get involved with the ladies in the office.

He went into one of the bathroom stalls and locked the door. Lifting one foot onto the toilet seat, he unlaced his sneaker.

"Is anybody here?" called Mr. Gates, the school janitor. The wheels on his big steel bucket squealed as he dragged it behind him. Apparently he was coming in to clean.

Gopher jumped onto the toilet seat. Through the crack between the door and the stall he could see Mr. Gates bending down, looking for feet.

Mr. Gates proceeded to dunk his mop into the dirty water, work the metal wringer on top, and swish the floor. When he came to Gopher's stall, he tried the door, but it wouldn't give. "Those kids!" he muttered. "Always locking 'em from the inside."

The next thing Gopher knew, the string mop was being swished here and there right beneath him. He wondered what Mr. Gates was going to do about the locked door. He hoped nothing, at least until he could get out of there.

Whistling tunelessly, Mr. Gates continued mopping for a few moments. Gopher looked through the crack again. Now Mr. Gates was shaking generous puffs of green-blue scouring powder into the sinks. It looked like he was done with the floor. Gopher got busy.

Perched unsteadily on the toilet seat, he removed the unlaced sneaker and held it in his hand. Then he started fishing in his pocket for the three dollars. It was a little tricky, balancing on the narrow toilet seat, holding the sneaker in one hand, and rummaging in his pocket with the other, all the time not making a sound. Gopher took a quick glance to see what the janitor was up to now. He was smearing some yellowy liquid all over the mirrors.

"Mr. Gates!" a boy's voice yelled loudly.

Plunk. Gopher was so startled he dropped the sneaker right into the toilet.

"Mr. Gates!" the voice yelled again. It was Kevin, calling from the doorway.

"Yeah?" Mr. Gates answered gruffly.

Gopher looked down at his sneaker floating in the water. Luckily, the last kid had flushed. He fished out the sneaker and held it an inch above the water to let it drain out as noiselessly

as possible. "Have you seen Gopher?" Kevin's voice continued. "Mrs. Morrison sent me to look for him."

"Nope, nobody's here," Mr. Gates answered without looking up. He was gathering together his supplies.

"Okay. I'll go look in the other boys' bathroom."

Mr. Gates got out his sign that showed the words WET FLOOR with a picture of somebody falling on his butt. He stood it by the door and left.

Gopher waited what seemed about five minutes. Once he was sure the janitor was gone for good, he got out the money and wadded it in the bottom of the cold, soggy shoe.

"Yuck," he said aloud as he wriggled his foot into the sneaker. Tying the wet laces wasn't any fun, either.

Checking once more to make sure that no one was around, he opened the stall door and took a step. *Squish.*

How was he going to explain *this*? he wondered. He grabbed a paper towel and tried to wipe the shoe dry. All he could do now was go back to class and hope for the best.

Step, *squish*, step, *squish*. Gopher proceeded down the hall. Well, at least he'd gotten the money back. A twinge of a smile played on his lips. And then he had another cheerful thought—if Fletcher tried to steal the money now, Gopher would be sure to tell him *how* it got wet.

The Search

At lunchtime there was the usual rush for everyone to get their jackets and lunch bags. Fletcher's eyes became big when he reached into his pocket and found the money missing. He elbowed Gopher in the ribs. "Did you steal the money out of my pocket?" he hissed.

"I didn't take it, I swear." Gopher held up his right hand, like they do on TV.

"Yeah? And yesterday you said you didn't have your milk money, either. You're lying."

"I'm not, I swear." Gopher didn't usually add all those "I swears" when he talked. Somehow lying made them necessary.

Fletcher came closer. Gopher was desperate. He racked his brain for something to take Fletcher's mind off the money. "What art project are you making these days?" he asked. "Something about a caveman again?"

Surprisingly, Fletcher hesitated, as if he was about to answer. Then he seemed to remember what he was doing. "None of your business," he snarled. "Give me back the money or I'll rearrange your face this afternoon when you're walking home from school."

"I don't have your money, I swear. I'm not the only kid in this school, you know."

"You're the only one who left the room since recess. Well, you and that Stephanie kid. She went to get the filmstrip. Maybe that's why she was gone so long."

Now Fletcher was accusing Stephanie? Gopher got so mad he started yelling. "You're really off your rocker if you think Stephanie took it!"

He decided he had to do *something* to convince Fletcher. He turned his right front pants pocket inside out. "Here, look. See? I don't have any money except my lousy twenty cents for milk. You want that?"

He held out the money, but Fletcher didn't take it.

"Keep going."

Gopher proceeded to turn out the rest of his pants pockets. Fletcher watched. "Okay, now your jacket."

Gopher obeyed. How far was Fletcher going to go with this thing? Gopher hadn't expected to undergo a full body search right here in the hallway.

After that was done, Fletcher reached his hand into Gopher's shirt pockets. Boy, what a mistake, getting Fletcher going.

Fletcher bent down and rummaged around the inside cuffs of Gopher's pants. Then he pulled up the pants legs and checked Gopher's socks. "I've heard of guys hiding stuff in their socks," he said.

Gopher began thinking of what he'd do when Fletcher ordered him to take off his shoes. He'd just make a run for it, he decided. What else could he do?

Fletcher stood up. "Well, I guess you don't

have it on you. You probably hid it in your desk. Don't think I won't check there the minute I get back from lunch. That's a promise." He started to walk away, and then he turned. "And I'll check that Stephanie kid's desk, too. That's another promise."

"You can't do that!" Gopher shouted. "Leave her out of this!" By the look on Fletcher's face, Gopher knew he'd made a mistake. Now Fletcher was even more suspicious.

"Oh, I get it. You and Stephanie are in this together. I heard her say you could copy her math paper. Since she'd do that, she'd probably steal the money, too."

"You're crazy!" shouted Gopher.

"Oh, no, I'm not," said Fletcher. "That dumb story about Mrs. Kelly losing the filmstrip— she made that up just to have more time."

Gopher was so furious he couldn't begin to answer. He had to hurt this guy somehow. He had to! He was just getting up his nerve to run at him and start hitting him when Mr. Swenson walked by.

"What are you boys still doing here? The lunch period started seven minutes ago. Get down to lunch—immediately!"

Mr. Swenson followed them to the end of the corridor. Gopher took the door that went to the lunchroom. Fletcher took the one going outside.

"What did I *do*?" groaned Gopher. Now Fletcher was going to start picking on Stephanie, too!

Three Dollars in a Pencil Box

"Did you go to Timbuktu, too?" Kevin asked as Gopher joined his group in the lunchroom. "You're late enough." Gopher mumbled something and began unwrapping his tuna fish sandwich. He wasn't very hungry.

Stephanie looked at him closely. "No milk *again*?" She pursed her lips in a certain way. "I say you got eggplant in there," she said, pointing to Gopher's head.

Gopher couldn't help grinning. "I have money," he answered softly. "I just didn't have time."

Stephanie changed back to her regular expression. "Here, have a milk." She plunked down a small blue carton in front of him.

"Thanks," he said. "But then what are you gonna drink?"

"Silly. I bought *two* milks. You've been so forgetful lately, I bought an extra one today."

"Gee, thanks." Gopher rummaged around in his pocket for the two dimes and held them out to her.

"Ah, just keep 'em. Maybe you'll need some extra for that tremendous valentine you're going to make." As usual, her smile made him feel better, if only a little.

After lunch Gopher found the papers in his desk all messed up. Fletcher had apparently kept his promise. Gopher looked to see what the sneak-ball was doing now. He was standing over Stephanie at her desk!

"Fletcher, these are *not* your three dollars," Stephanie was saying. "I brought them in this morning. I'm going to buy my valentines on the way home from school."

All the kids started gathering around. "What do you want from Stephanie?" Brenda demanded.

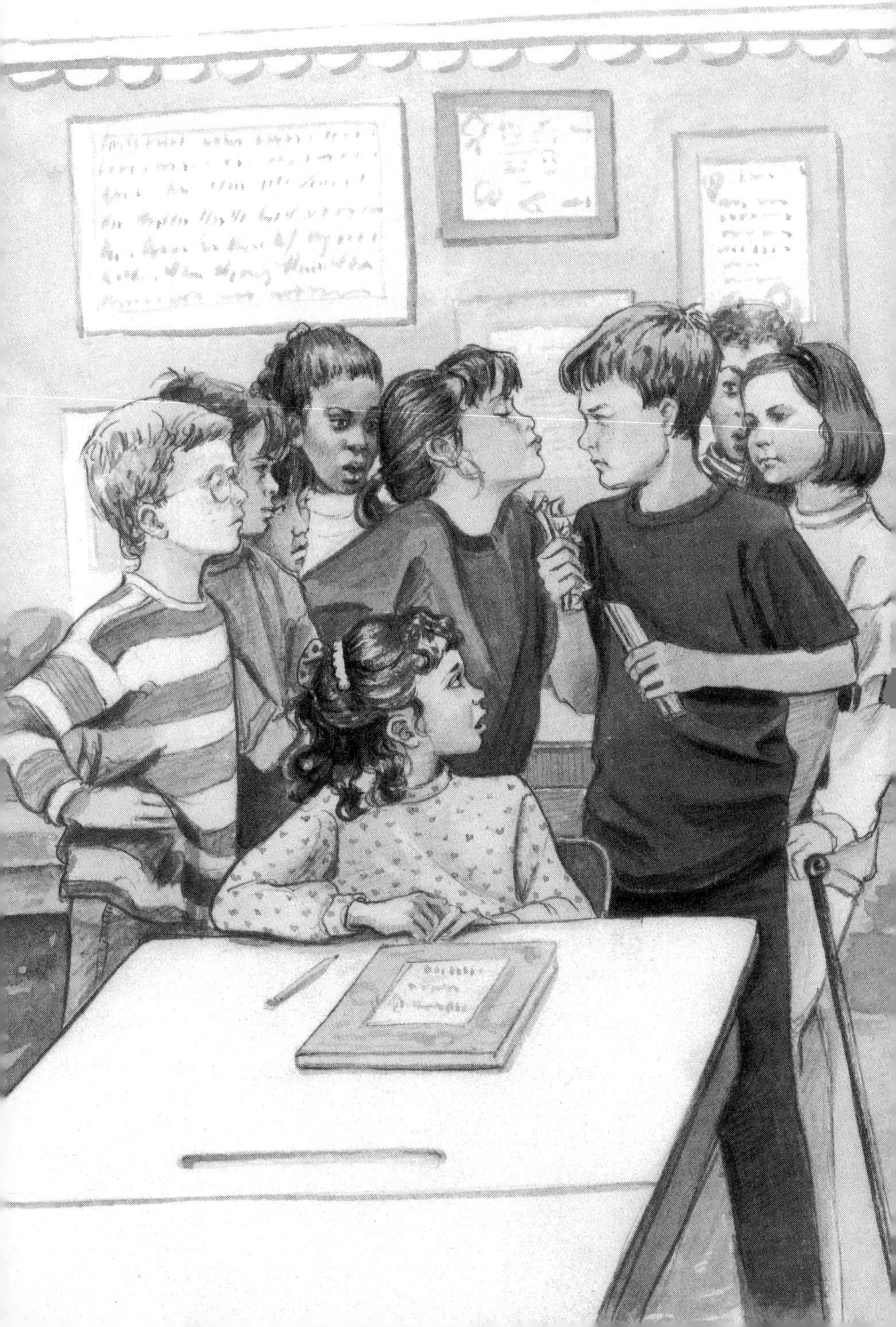

"Uh, I had three dollars in my pocket this morning, and now they're gone," Fletcher complained, not too forcefully. He held up three folded dollar bills in one hand and Stephanie's red pencil box in the other. "I found these three dollars right here in Stephanie's pencil box. When she went to get the filmstrip this morning, she took the money out of my pocket. She must have put it in here while nobody was looking."

"Did Stephanie *say* you could look in her pencil box?" Brenda wanted to know.

"Well, no."

"And besides, if Stephanie says she didn't take your money, she didn't take it. You understand . . . buster?" Brenda put her face a few inches from Fletcher's.

Fletcher turned away. "Well . . . "

Everyone started ganging up on him. "Fletcher, you're a jerk."

"You've got a lot of nerve—going into Stephanie's desk without asking."

"And even worse, accusing her of stealing!"

"Okay, okay, everybody," said Stephanie. "This is between Fletcher and me. Don't get excited."

She turned to Fletcher. "I'm sorry someone took your money, Fletcher, but it wasn't me." She gently removed the three dollars and the pencil box from his hands. "This is *my* money." She looked him in the eyes.

Everybody waited. Nobody said anything. Nobody moved away. Fletcher looked around at all the unfriendly faces.

"Well, I don't think those were my three dollars anyway," he said at last. "My money was folded in a different way." He turned and walked back to his seat.

Everybody was still out of their seats when Mrs. Morrison walked in. "Class?" she asked. "What's happening?"

Brenda explained how Fletcher had accused Stephanie of taking his money, that he had even rummaged through her desk looking for it.

"Fletcher, is that true?" Mrs. Morrison's eyes were very narrow.

"Well . . . " Fletcher looked down and twisted his mouth for a long moment.

Mrs. Morrison exploded. "Fletcher, your behavior is becoming more and more impossible! I think you owe Stephanie an apology."

Fletcher stared at the floor some more. Mrs. Morrison, and all the kids, waited.

"I'm sorry," Fletcher finally mumbled to nobody in particular. Stephanie said something about it being okay.

"Fletcher, go sit down!" From her tone of voice Mrs. Morrison might have been scolding a dog who had wet the living room rug. "And let me tell you, young man, if this happens one more time . . . " She didn't finish her sentence. With the you'd-better-watch-out look she gave Fletcher, she didn't have to.

The Note

"Please, class, take out your language books," said Mrs. Morrison. Gopher got out his language book, but his head was spinning. Stephanie had simply *told* Fletcher he couldn't have the money! She had even taken it right out of his hand!

"Today we're going to review adverbs." Mrs. Morrison's voice sounded a thousand miles away. Who cared about adverbs? Stephanie had stood up to Fletcher Simpson! And she wasn't even particularly brave! She certainly wasn't like Brenda.

Gopher looked over at Stephanie. With her curly black hair and her cute nose and her braces, she was so . . . so "girl-looking." How could *she* tell Fletcher what to do?

"Okay, who wants to tell us the difference between an adverb and an adjective?" asked Mrs. Morrison. "Remember we talked about this yesterday?"

Not one hand went up.

"Class, now really!" Mrs. Morrison waited, hands on hips, her face set in an expectant look.

Still, not one hand.

Finally, Stephanie raised her hand a few inches.

"Good, Stephanie. I knew I could count on you."

Stephanie said she thought adverbs talk about verbs and adjectives talk about nouns. "But maybe it's the other way around," she added.

"No, that's perfectly correct, Stephanie. I just wish the others had been paying as much attention as you."

All of Gopher's emotions centered on Stephanie. She was so smart—she even knew what an adverb was. But more than that, she was so brave! She had taken the pencil case right out of Fletcher's hand!

Mrs. Morrison began passing out mimeographed papers with blanks on them. "Okay, class, fill in the blanks with an appropriate word and then write whether that word is an adverb or an adjective." Even Mrs. Morrison sounded like she didn't like this stuff much.

Oh, if only *he* could stand up to Fletcher like Stephanie had, thought Gopher. There she was, busily filling in the blanks. *She* didn't have a care in the world. He decided to do something.

He took out a piece of yellow paper with thin blue lines. He wrote:

Dear Fletcher—

He stopped. That "dear" was definitely *not* what he wanted to say. He crumpled up the paper and took another sheet. He started again.

Fletcher—

That was better. He chewed on his pencil lightly. Now, what should he say? He started writing.

I took the money. You stole it from me. I stole it back. If you want it, you'll have to beat me up for it. I'll be waiting for you under the big tree after school.

Gopher

Gopher wrote Fletcher's name on the outside of the note. "Pass it on," he whispered to the boy in back of him. It went from hand to hand and finally arrived at Fletcher's desk. He opened it and read. He gave Gopher a mean, nasty scowl.

For the rest of the afternoon Gopher nervously watched the red second hand of the big white clock whiz round and round. Usually it went so slowly. Today it seemed like only five minutes had passed when the final bell rang.

He plodded to the hallway to pick up his jacket. He couldn't see any reason to hurry.

When he got to his coathook, Fletcher was putting on his jacket. He shoved one arm in the sleeve, purposely hitting Gopher in the stomach. Then he turned around and did the same thing with the other arm. "Hey, I said under the tree," protested Gopher, "not here."

"Okay, squirt, whatever you say. And why don't you bring your brother, too? He can call the ambulance to take you home."

"Oh, yeah?" said Gopher, trying to sound brave.

"Yeah," snarled Fletcher. "I gotta go home for a couple of minutes, then I'll be back." He started walking toward the door. "And in the meantime you'd better look at yourself in the mirror. You'll never look the same again after I'm done with you."

Waiting

Gopher moved his tongue around his mouth. He toyed with a tooth. How could it be loose already? That yucky taste—it couldn't be blood, could it? He felt his nose. No, it wasn't broken, *yet*.

Was he being just plain stupid, saying he'd meet Fletcher under the big tree all by himself? When Stephanie had stood up to Fletcher, she'd been in the classroom, with all the kids around. This was different. Boy, was it ever!

Gopher debated going back into the classroom and telling Mrs. Morrison. Or maybe he'd go get Kevin to come with him.

No, he had to go through with it. By himself.

If he didn't, things would go on just the same—
Fletcher bullying him around all the time, and
he, Gopher, taking it. Anyway, the damage
was already done. Fletcher was steaming mad
at him. No use backing out now.

He wondered if he should put on his jacket.
It *was* cold, and the jacket might absorb some
of the punches. Still, his mom wouldn't be
happy if he came home with it ruined. He
decided he'd put it on but he wouldn't zip it.
That way he could get it out of harm's way
quickly when the time came.

He walked outside. The money inside his
still-damp sneaker felt a little funny. How was
he going to get it out to give to Fletcher if he
was beaten up real bad? Well, he'd worry
about that later . . . if he had to.

He walked toward the big tree. Fletcher
wasn't there yet. Where could he be? He probably went home to go to the bathroom, thought
Gopher. All of a sudden Gopher had to go to
the bathroom, too. Badly. The more he

thought about it, the more he had to go. He paced back and forth. He kept watching the street for Fletcher.

"Hey, Gopher, you wanna come over after?" It was Kevin, riding past on his bike.

"Nah, I gotta go make the valentine," Gopher answered.

"Well, why aren't you making it, then?" Kevin asked. "What are you wasting your time around here for?"

Gopher wondered the same thing.

"Remember, make it really *big*," Kevin called over his shoulder.

Fletcher still didn't come. Now Gopher could hardly stand it, he had to go to the bathroom so badly. He could probably make it to the bathroom and back before Fletcher got there. Maybe he should risk it. He looked down the street toward Fletcher's house. What was that guy doing?

Then Gopher had a horrible thought. Maybe Fletcher had gone home to get a knife! Fletcher always talked about his brother.

Maybe he was going to do the same thing his brother had done!

Gopher swallowed hard and shifted from one foot to the other. He guessed he'd zip up his jacket after all. It'd be pretty hard to get a knife through that shiny material—unless the knife was really sharp.

Would Fletcher use the *same* knife his brother had used? Gopher wondered. Nah, he didn't think so. They didn't let guys keep the knives they stabbed people with. He'd seen a picture in the paper of a whole table covered with knives and guns that the police had taken away from criminals. They always took the knife away.

Gopher felt slightly better, but only for a moment. So what if they'd taken the knife away? There were plenty of knives. Fletcher could grab any old one. Gopher took a deep breath and let it out slowly. When he had written the note, he certainly hadn't thought of the knife.

But, nah, Fletcher wouldn't come at him

with a weapon. A kid doesn't come at another kid with a knife. Does he? Gopher dimly remembered hearing about a kid in Texas who was only nine, who had shot another kid on the school playground with his father's hunting rifle.

By this time all the school buses had left. A few cars had been waiting to pick up children, but now they had gone, too. Gopher waited. After a while even the teachers started to leave. The place was just about deserted now.

Maybe that was what Fletcher had in mind! He'd wait until everyone went home and then there'd be no one around to interfere. Gopher rubbed his hands together and looked around. Mrs. Morrison's car was still there. If he was knocked unconscious and was bleeding to death, at least she'd find him, probably.

Another teacher got into her car and left. Gopher wished he knew what time it was. It seemed like he'd been waiting for hours.

Gopher blew on his hands. He was really

getting cold. Maybe that sneakball wouldn't even show up, he thought angrily. But it was stupid to be angry about that. He *hoped* he wouldn't show up. Or did he? If Fletcher didn't show up, would that mean he'd chickened out, or just that he just wanted to put it off until another day?

After a few more minutes Gopher saw Mrs. Morrison come out of the building. She was walking with another fifth-grade teacher, Mrs. Riley. Mrs. Morrison waved, hesitated, and then started walking over to him. When he realized what she was doing, he started walking, too.

"Matthew?" she asked in a concerned voice. "What are you still doing here?"

"I'm waiting for someone." Gopher looked back at the big tree. "But I guess he's not coming."

"Oh, that's too bad. Is there anything I can do?"

"No," said Gopher, shrugging helplessly.

"You're sure? I could give you a ride home. Mrs. Riley and I are going shopping at the mall. Your house is on our way."

"No, it's okay. Thanks anyway."

"Well, if you're sure." Mrs. Morrison turned to leave. "Bye then. See you tomorrow. Don't forget—tomorrow's Valentine's Day."

"No, I won't." Actually, worrying about Fletcher, he had sort of forgotten. He didn't feel much like making a "tremendous" valentine anymore.

He waited a few more minutes, but by now it was pretty obvious that Fletcher wasn't going to show up. He might as well go home.

As he passed the yellow house with green shutters he looked for Fletcher, but there was no sign of him. Gopher just couldn't figure it out.

He walked a while and then he realized something. He, Gopher, *had* shown up. He'd been prepared to take whatever Fletcher dished out. He had stood up to that obnoxious bully after all. Sort of.

Buying Red Velvet

Gopher walked into his house. He'd forgotten how badly he had to go to the bathroom. After he took care of that, he removed the money from his sneaker and put it in his pocket. He grabbed a powdered-sugar donut and let the outside door slam behind him.

As he pedaled off on his bike he took a bite of donut. Usually that taste was about the most delicious he could imagine—those powdery sugar crystals mixed with the fresh-bread flavor of the donut itself. Today, he might as well have been eating cardboard.

At the mall he went to the fabric store first. He'd start the valentine with a background of red velvet.

"May I help you?" asked the saleslady. Apparently she thought it was a little unusual for a ten-year-old boy to be looking at fabrics.

"Yes," said Gopher. "I think I'll buy about two yards of red velvet, please."

"Are you sure?" asked the lady. "It does cost twelve ninety-five a yard, you know."

$12.95 a yard! Gopher had had no idea. How could *anything* cost $12.95 a yard? "Do you have anything cheaper?" he asked.

"Well, we do have some red flannel on sale. It's only two ninety-nine a yard. Would you like two yards of that?"

Rats! What was he going to do? He couldn't even afford one yard of cheap red flannel, not if he was going to have any money left over for the stuff to go on it. He'd have to make his valentine out of red paper instead.

Gopher thanked the lady and went to the dime store. As he walked in he saw Mrs. Morrison and Mrs. Riley at the checkout counter. "Hi, Mrs. Morrison. Hi, Mrs. Riley," he called.

"Well, Matthew!" said Mrs. Morrison,

looking very surprised. "This is the second time we meet after school today, isn't it?"

"That will be five fifty-two," said the saleslady as she handed Mrs. Morrison a big blue bag with the store's name on it. Gopher waited while Mrs. Morrison paid. The lady started ringing up Mrs. Riley's order. Mrs. Riley was buying a lot of red and white lopsided balls. Gopher wondered what she needed that stuff for.

"Well, see you tomorrow," he said after a minute.

"Yes, tomorrow," answered Mrs. Morrison, sounding a little strange.

Gopher went to the crafts counter and started looking around. Everything here was also a lot more expensive than he'd been counting on. He'd need $1.50 just for the poster board. That would leave only $1.50 for all the other stuff.

What should he buy? There were sequins in gold and silver and other colors, shiny beads, packages of ribbon. But everything cost about a dollar. He wouldn't have enough money to buy more than one thing.

Gopher considered giving up on the whole project and just going to the card shop to *buy* a valentine. But he remembered the who'd-want-a-valentine-like-that face Brenda had made when she'd announced the project to the class. No, he'd simply have to do the best he could.

He walked around a little more. He stopped at a special display of candy valentine hearts. He had always liked those hearts with the funny sayings on them. *Sweet stuff,* said an orange one. *Not tonight,* said a green one. *Hot mama,* said a pink one. Maybe he could glue those around the valentine. At least that would be kind of funny. He looked at the price tag— $1.39. Too expensive.

He went back to the crafts counter. He had to have something big. After all, this was going to be a *big* valentine. When he happened upon the paper doilies, he knew he had his answer.

The twelve doilies in the package were a

little smaller than the dinner plates at home. They should cover the whole thing, he decided. And the price was okay—$1.49. The poster board and the doilies together would cost $2.99. He'd have one penny left over. Luckily he had gold paint and Q-tips at home. He didn't need to buy those.

He took his purchases to the checkout counter. "I bet I know what you're making with these," the cashier teased. "You're making a valentine, right?"

"Yes. For my teacher."

"Lucky teacher." The lady was punching all kinds of numbers into the cash register. She ripped off the receipt and started putting the items into a large bag. "That will be three dollars and seventeen cents," she said.

"There must be some mistake," said Gopher politely. "I added it up, and I got two ninety-nine." He didn't like contradicting a grown-up, but after all, he *had* added it up. Besides, all he had was three dollars.

"Yes, but there's tax." Gopher had forgotten

the tax! Now what? He'd have to start all over. But the sequins and beads and ribbons were even *more* expensive, at least for the little amount you got. He was just about to go back to the crafts counter to try to figure this all out when he put his hand in his pocket in one last desperate search for a solution. He felt something. The two dimes from lunch! Stephanie had told him he might need them.

He paid the bill and headed home. Finding those two dimes made him feel that at least Stephanie was on his side. Maybe this valentine wouldn't be such a disaster after all.

The Red-Faced
Fat Lady

Gopher arrived home and began working on his valentine right away. He taped the two pieces of poster board together from the back. Now at least his valentine would be *big* enough. After making a practice heart out of newspaper, he cut the poster-board one. He had his heart.

Gopher tore open the package of doilies. He laid the doilies flat around the outside of the giant heart, sticking out from the back. That looked like something a first-grader would do. He put one doily in the middle of the heart and arranged all the other doilies around it. That wasn't much better. Maybe doilies weren't such a great idea after all.

He tried cutting a doily in half and folding it in ridges, kind of like a Japanese fan. That looked better. He did that to all the doilies. These he stapled as evenly as he could all around the edge of the valentine. It didn't look quite as good as he had hoped. Maybe when he added the gold paint . . .

With a pencil he outlined a smaller heart inside the bigger one. Inside the smaller heart, in his best handwriting, he wrote, *To the Best Teacher in the World*. Carefully dipping a Q-tip into the small jar of gold paint, he went over the penciling. That was it. He was finished. He stood back to look.

What a disappointment! It didn't look at all like he had imagined. It was just a red piece of paper with white doilies and gold writing. Big deal! What would the kids say when they saw it?

Maybe if he added more stuff . . . He *could* use his own money to go back and buy the candy hearts and the ribbon. He'd sort of been saving that money to buy a new paintbrush, but, geez, he just couldn't go to school tomorrow with such a plain, ordinary valentine.

He went to the top drawer of his bureau and

took out the copper-colored tin box. "One, two, three, four . . . " He had to take a little extra to make sure he had enough for the tax. That would leave a little over a dollar in the tin box. After all, he didn't want to spend *all* his money.

"Back again?" said the lady at the dime store.

"Yeah," said Gopher. He never knew how to answer when a grown-up asked him a question like that.

"That should be *some* valentine. I wish someone would give me one like that."

"Yeah," said Gopher again. He didn't mean to be rude, but he wasn't at all sure that it would be "some" valentine. He sure hoped the candy hearts and ribbon did the trick.

When he got home, he opened the package of candy hearts and got out his bottle of glue. Wouldn't Fletcher be happy to see how much trouble he was having! One by one, he glued on the hearts. *Be Mine* went next to *Dream Girl*. *Cool* and *Kiss Me* found their various spots.

Next the ribbon. He twisted and pulled and curled and tied, but that ribbon just wouldn't cooperate. He finally managed to get it to stay in some kind of a big loopy mess. This he stapled to the top of the heart. Now he was really done. He couldn't think of anything else to do. He looked at his valentine.

At first it looked like a poster-board valentine with pastel-colored candy hearts stuck here and there all over the front and doily fans sticking out all around the edges. Then, as he looked some more, it began to look like a red-faced fat lady with pimples all over her face and white tufts of hair sticking out all around her head. The ribbon looked like an enormous hair bow right in the middle of her forehead. What a mess!

Gopher took the valentine downstairs to show his mother. "What do you think of it?" he asked. He was almost smiling. The valentine had come out *so* bad that it actually looked kind of funny. Still, it would not be funny tomorrow when he had to show it to his classmates.

When his mother saw the valentine, her face took on a peculiar expression. It looked as if she was trying to decide if it would be all right to laugh. Gopher stiffened his eyebrows. The peculiar expression on his mother's face disappeared.

"It's great," she said without enthusiasm.

"You don't really think it's great, do you?" All of a sudden Gopher could see nothing funny about the valentine, nothing at all.

"Well, honey, maybe it's not great, but it's fine." That was even worse. *Fine* was an all-purpose word grown-ups used when you did something that wasn't very good, but they knew it was the best you could do.

"I think your classmates should be very grateful to you. You worked hard, you even spent your own money. Take heart, honey. You did your best. Now it's time for bed, okay?"

As he was getting his pajamas on, Gopher looked again at the valentine. Maybe it didn't look *that* much like a red-faced fat lady with pimples and white hair, but it still wasn't very good. Gopher had to agree with his mother. His valentine was only "fine."

Fletcher, the Same and Different

The valentine only looked "fine" in the morning, too. Gopher got dressed and came down to breakfast. "Happy Valentine's Day, love," said his mother. She leaned over and kissed him on the forehead. "Here's a little present for you."

She gave him a small heart-shaped box of candy. "Aw, Mom." In all the commotion he had forgotten to buy his own parents a valentine. "Sorry, I forgot."

"Don't worry about it," she answered lightly. "I know how hard you worked on the valentine. That was a very generous thing to do. Having such a generous son is enough valentine for your dad and me."

Gopher gave her a hug. "Thanks, Mom."

After breakfast he carefully packed up the valentine in a big plastic bag and started out for school. He was a little nervous about walking past Fletcher's house, but not too much. If Fletcher had something in mind, he had something in mind, too. That dirt bag was *not* going to get this valentine, no matter what. Besides, Gopher secretly hoped, maybe he wouldn't even show up.

But, unlike the afternoon before, Fletcher showed up. As Gopher approached the yellow house with green shutters, there he was, waiting in his usual spot. Gopher braced himself.

"Hey, Gopher, what are you carrying in the bag—your lunch?" Fletcher's voice had that same singsongy tone Gopher couldn't stand.

"The class valentine," Gopher answered, as calmly as he could.

"Humph," scoffed Fletcher, making a grab for the bag. "I'm sure it's really stupid, but let me see it."

Gopher managed to yank the bag out of Fletcher's reach just in time. He placed the bag on the ground and planted both feet on the plastic, being careful not to stand on the valentine itself. "You get this valentine only after you beat me up so bad I can't stand up any longer." He crossed his arms across his chest—he was not going to be bullied around anymore.

Fletcher stood there, confused and speechless. "Yeah?" He punched Gopher lightly on the chest.

Gopher didn't flinch. He glowered at Fletcher and held his ground.

"You mean you're not going to fight?" said Fletcher.

Gopher was determined not to get drawn in. He stood there, as unmovable as the SLOW—CHILDREN sign Fletcher was standing beside.

Fletcher circled around. Gopher followed him with his eyes but made no attempt to defend himself. "Is this the way your big brother fights?" taunted Fletcher. "Wimp. Wimp. Wimp."

Gopher didn't say a word. Fletcher rabbit-punched him on the arm, the back, the chest. "C'mon, *fight*," he ordered. But again, no response from Gopher.

For a couple more minutes Fletcher fumed and pranced. Several times he brought his clenched fist close to Gopher's face and made a sneering noise. Gopher steadied himself and waited.

After a while, when Fletcher's fit was finally over, Gopher picked up the valentine and started walking away.

Fletcher watched him go, and then he raced to catch up with him. Gopher hid the valentine behind his back and waited to see what Fletcher was going to do this time.

"Say," said Fletcher, as if an idea had just occurred to him, "you didn't really show up yesterday, did you?"

"I showed up."

"You did?"

"*I* did," Gopher answered. "*You* didn't."

"Yeah, that was a bummer. My dad wouldn't let me out of the house. Said I had to clean up my mess in the workroom."

That sounded like a pretty weak excuse to Gopher, but he let it go.

"Anyway, I was so sure you'd chicken out. . . . You're kidding, right? You didn't come, really?"

Gopher set his face to show he'd already answered that question.

Fletcher shook his head in disbelief. "Boy, I never expected that!"

Sensing that the conversation was over, Gopher started walking again. Surprisingly, Fletcher fell into step with him.

"So tell me, how *did* the valentine turn out?" For the first time Gopher could remember, Fletcher wasn't using that singsongy voice.

"It came out okay," Gopher answered flatly.

"Did it cost a lot? Those projects always cost more than you think."

Gopher couldn't figure out why Fletcher was acting this way. It was as if he was actually trying to be *nice*. "Yeah, it cost a lot," he answered.

For a few moments the two boys walked in uncomfortable silence. "I've got a project at home that I've been wanting to bring in and show the class, too," Fletcher said finally.

"Yeah?" In spite of himself, Gopher couldn't help being a *little* interested. Fletcher's projects were always so unusual.

"You know my brother? The one who was chosen senior-class artist?"

"I've heard about him. He's in jail, right?"

Fletcher faltered. "Kinda," he said, brushing the comment aside. "Well, he built this caveman computer."

"Yeah, I've seen it. I walked over to the high school."

"You did?" Fletcher was obviously pleased. "Anyway, that gave me an idea, and I built a caveman television set."

Gopher nodded.

"Yeah, it turned out really good!" Fletcher was actually smiling as he talked. "I got some wood and painted it to look like rocks and I cut out a hole for the picture. And then for the programs I made rolls of cartoons—with caveman characters and caveman houses and caveman everything."

"I'd like to see it," said Gopher, forgetting it was Fletcher he was talking to.

"Yeah, Ms. Connors said she'd *love* to see it!" Fletcher looked down, the happiness gone from his face. "But I don't have anybody to help me carry it to school."

"That's too bad." Gopher didn't know what else to say.

They had almost reached the schoolyard by now. Even though Gopher felt a little relieved that Fletcher seemed to want to be nice now, he still didn't want kids to see them walking to school together. "Well, I gotta go," he said, hoping Fletcher would get the hint. "I gotta take this valentine to the furnace room so the kids can sign it."

"Yeah," said Fletcher, not leaving.

"So long, then," said Gopher, beginning to walk away.

"Ah, Gopher?" called Fletcher, and then he stopped.

"Yeah?"

Fletcher scuffed the ground and cleared his throat a couple of times. Finally he began. "Do you think . . . you know, since you walk past my house anyway, that someday . . . you know, that maybe next week, when you don't have the valentine to worry about or anything . . . that maybe you could help me carry the caveman television to school?" He looked at Gopher for a fleeting second. "I'd really like the kids to see it . . . or at least Ms. Connors."

Gopher was so surprised by Fletcher's request that he couldn't answer right away.

"I could load it on my wagon," said Fletcher. "It wouldn't be heavy."

"Well . . . "

"I'll pay you," offered Fletcher.

Fletcher's forlorn expression reminded

Gopher of a scrawny, homeless cat who sometimes came meowing around his backyard. How could he *not* feel sorry for a guy who didn't have a single friend to help him with a small job like this? "Nah, you don't have to do that," he said.

Gopher weighed the pros and cons. It wasn't a big deal. And maybe doing it would convince Fletcher to keep on being nice. Besides, if he wanted to see the caveman television set, this might be his only chance.

Still . . . it *was* Fletcher Simpson who was asking.

"Okay," he said at last, reluctantly.

"Radical!" cheered Fletcher, pounding a fist into his palm.

The Underwhelming Reaction

Gopher didn't have any more time to think about Fletcher because just then Kevin, Lance, and Brenda ran up to him. "Let's see it!" they shouted together.

"I don't want to open it out *here*," said Gopher. "Mrs. Morrison might be looking out the window."

"Can't we just have a peek?" asked Brenda, grabbing the valentine from inside the bag. When she had removed it, she looked at it in amazement. "Is *that* what it's going to look like?"

"Geez, Gopher," added Lance. "Did a hurricane happen in the candy-hearts factory? They're all over the place!"

"Did you have to use those doilies?" threw in Brenda.

"Hey, guys, take it easy," said Kevin. "Gopher tried his best."

Brenda scowled at the valentine some more. "Maybe we should have gone with the store-bought card after all."

"Sure, Brenda, rub it in," said Kevin, getting more and more excited. "Like every project *you* make turns out just great. Remember your diorama of Niagara Falls? Huh? How it looked like you were trying to suffocate your pet rock collection with plastic wrap?"

"Well, yours of Mount Rushmore wasn't any better," replied Brenda. "It looked like four overfed rats with a skin condition. You even said so yourself."

Even though Gopher appreciated Kevin's sticking up for him, if what Kevin was saying could be called that, he really wasn't enjoying this. "I'm taking this to the furnace room," he said. "I'll leave some gold paint and some Q-tips nearby. Tell kids to come sign, *if* they want to."

"Of course we want to," said Kevin, looking meaningfully at Brenda.

"Oh, all right," complained Brenda. "I'll go tell the kids. Lance, you tell some, too. I don't know why everybody expects *me* to do all the work around here."

Gopher put the valentine back in the bag and started walking toward the building. He saw Brenda talking to some girls by the swings. She was covering her mouth with her hand, so Gopher couldn't hear what she was saying. Still, when they all started looking at him and giggling, he *knew* what she was saying. He felt like going over there and smashing the valentine over her head. Instead he took it to the furnace room.

Several kids came in immediately to start signing their names. "Where are we supposed to sign with all these candy hearts all over the place?" somebody asked.

"Is this all the stuff you could get for three *whole* dollars?" demanded another kid.

All morning one kid after another asked to leave the room on some made-up reason. Gopher knew they were going down to sign the valentine. When they got back, he watched to see if they had any message for him. Did they like it? Did they hate it? They didn't have to come to his desk and *tell* him what they thought about it. They could just give the okay sign from across the room.

Or they could send a note. Kids were always sending notes. Here he had practically killed himself making this dumb valentine, and not one kid cared enough to even send him a note. Well, that was the last time he'd ever make anything for these kids again!

A few minutes before recess, the boy behind Gopher tapped him on the shoulder. "A note," he whispered.

Well, it was about time! Gopher opened it. It read:

> *Gopher—*
> *Your valentine didn't come out as*
> *good as you hoped, did it?*
>
> > *Fletcher*

So, Fletcher wasn't done making fun of him after all!

Reading that note unleashed the anger that had been building up in Gopher all morning. He was furious! He was furious at his classmates, who didn't show any appreciation for his work. He was furious at the people who made red velvet and charged so much for it. He was furious at himself for wasting all his time and money on this stupid valentine and not even remembering to give his parents one.

And now this!

He took out a piece of yellow paper. In huge letters he scribbled: *BUG OFF!!!*

He wrote Fletcher's name on the outside and told the kid behind him to pass it on. Boy, here that creep had pretended he'd changed—just to get Gopher to help him carry his dumb caveman television to school. Ha! As if Gopher would help him carry anything, anyplace, anytime, for as long as he lived! He hoped Fletcher's caveman television got eaten by ancient, dinosaur-sized termites!

"Another note," said the boy behind him. It was from Fletcher again.

Gopher—

*I can help you make it better. Meet
me under the big tree during recess.*

> *Fletcher*

Gopher turned and looked at Fletcher. Was
this some kind of a joke? Maybe Fletcher had
decided to beat him up after all. Well, Gopher
had given him one chance—two, if you
counted this morning. He wasn't going to give
him another!

"Time for recess, class," said Mrs. Morrison.
"If some of you want to stay in and help me
put up red and white streamers, I'd appre-
ciate it."

Most of the kids, but not Gopher, got excited. "Red and white streamers! That must
mean a party!"

"That's right," said Mrs. Morrison. "You've
been so good lately, I've decided to surprise
you with a Valentine's Day party. I have some
streamers right here." She reached into a large

blue bag, the same one that Gopher had seen her carrying at the dime store the day before. "Oh, dear, the streamers don't seem to be here."

She called for Gopher. "Matthew, please go ask Mrs. Riley if she happened to get my streamers by mistake. We were both so surprised to see you yesterday, I think we got ourselves mixed up."

"Okay," he said, starting to leave.

"Oh, and Matthew, be sure not to let the class hear. I don't think Mrs. Riley's going to tell her class about their party until after lunch."

Gopher did as he was told. In a few minutes he was back with two rolls of red streamers and two rolls of white. So *this* was the red and white stuff that looked like lopsided balls!

"Thank goodness!" said Mrs. Morrison. "Did you have any trouble asking her so the class wouldn't hear?"

"I guess she decided to tell them early. They're all excited about a party, too."

"Okay, now," said Mrs. Morrison, "those who want to go to recess are free to leave. Those who want to stay and put up streamers and do other things to help with the party may do so."

It wasn't hard for Gopher to decide which he wanted to do. He had had enough of valentine decorations! He walked toward the door.

"Wait up, Gopher," someone called. It was Robin. "I'm *so* glad Mrs. Morrison decided to give us a party," she said. "You know, it was my job to buy the food. You wouldn't believe how little food three dollars can buy. All I was able to get was one lollipop apiece and a medium-size bag of potato chips. Some party!"

"I know just what you mean," said Gopher. He explained how the valentine wasn't anything like he had planned, either.

"Well, it doesn't matter. Now that Mrs. Morrison is giving us a party, who cares if the valentine turned out a little ... " She shrugged.

"Yeah, who cares?"

Robin joined the other girls on the playground, and Gopher started walking around. He glanced toward the big tree, the one where Fletcher had said he'd meet him. Fletcher was standing there. He lifted his hand in a sort of hello. Then he gestured that Gopher should come.

Now what? This Fletcher was all over the place—first he was nasty, then nice, then nasty. Was he about to be nice again?

Gopher didn't care enough to find out. He turned to walk away, but Fletcher called to him. "Hurry up, Gopher, we don't have much time."

Much time to do *what*? To get beaten bloody? No thanks. Gopher continued walking.

The next thing he knew, Fletcher was beside him, tapping him on the shoulder.

Fletcher Runs Home

"What do you want?" Gopher asked. He wasn't in the mood to be friendly.

"I have a great idea," said Fletcher. "I heard the kids making fun of your valentine, and I thought of a way to make it better."

"You heard the kids making fun? What about your note? You were making fun yourself!"

"No, I wasn't!" Fletcher was indignant. "I just said your valentine didn't turn out as good as you hoped. What's wrong with that?"

"What's *wrong*? You were rubbing it in."

"No, I wasn't. But then you wrote back, 'bug off.' And you walked away just now. You sure are a hard guy to help."

"*Help?* What do you mean?"

"I mean *help*," Fletcher replied. "Didn't you read my second note, the one where I said I could help you make it better?"

Gopher grunted. Maybe he had made a mistake after all.

"Anyway, we're wasting time. Recess is only fifteen minutes, you know."

"I know," said Gopher. He sure didn't know what that had to do with his valentine, though.

"Well, you remember my caveman Christmas tree?" continued Fletcher. "How I had those colored beads, and I pretended they were electric lights and all?"

"Yeah?" said Gopher. He remembered Fletcher's caveman Christmas tree very well.

"Well, I was thinking, I've got some beads left over and maybe you could glue them on the valentine, and maybe then everyone would like it better. I kinda know how it feels when kids don't like your art project."

Gopher knew Fletcher was talking about the Christmas art contest, where this same caveman Christmas tree had received only four votes.

"Well, anyway," said Fletcher, "as I said, I've got these beads left over. Why don't you try gluing some on the valentine? It might help."

Gopher considered, and then he said, "Thanks anyway, but it's too late. We're going to give Mrs. Morrison the valentine right after lunch. When would we have time to glue them on?" Gopher realized after he'd said it that he had used the word *we.*

Then he realized something else. Of all the kids in the class, Fletcher was the only one who understood about the valentine—how it cost a lot more than he had planned, and how disappointing it was that it hadn't turned out like he'd wanted, and how much it hurt when kids made fun of it.

"It's not too late," Fletcher almost shouted. "I could run home right now and get the stuff, and then we could work on it during lunch. I don't have to eat at home. I could bring a sandwich."

Then Gopher remembered something. "No, you'd better not do that. It's against the rules to leave the playground during recess. If they see you, you'll get in trouble. And if you're not back in time, look out! Mrs. Morrison's already on your case about Stephanie's money."

"I'll be back in time." Fletcher sounded insulted that Gopher should think he couldn't do what he said he could. He began racing toward his house before Gopher could say another word.

Gopher walked around the schoolyard in a daze. Was this really happening? Was Fletcher Simpson really running like a wild man to try to help Gopher? Fletcher would be in big trouble if he got caught . . . and he knew it.

The school bell rang. Recess was over. As all the kids lined up at the door Gopher looked toward the yellow house with green shutters. "Okay, kids, everybody back to class," said the playground aide. Gopher walked into the building. Fletcher hadn't gotten back in time.

Mrs. Riley
to the Rescue

"Come to order, class," said Mrs. Morrison as everyone entered the classroom. "I know you're all excited about the party, but there's still another hour until lunch. Let's make good use of the time."

The classroom continued to bustle. Brenda was still telling the streamers committee where to put the last two streamers. Kevin and Joshua were setting out paper cups on a large silver-colored tray. Stephanie was arranging paper napkins with valentine designs on a big round table. Elizabeth and Nadia were following her, placing one pink cupcake and several pieces of candy onto each napkin. Eric, Orlando, and Brooke were cutting out red hearts and taping them here and there around the room. Gary and Shawn were throwing erasers. In all the confusion, Fletcher's absence had not been noticed.

Gopher looked out the window in the direction of Fletcher's house. No sign of him. If Fletcher came back before Mrs. Morrison got serious about getting the class to sit down, he'd be okay. Otherwise . . . at the very least, he wouldn't be able to come to the party, Gopher figured.

"Hey, where's Fletcher?" called out Brenda. She wanted Cindy to put a streamer onto a wooden molding above the blackboard but Cindy was too short. "Somebody get Fletcher," Brenda yelled again. "He's tall, he can do it."

"Fletcher will be back in a minute," said Gopher. "He had to go to the office or something." He hoped that "or something" covered leaving the schoolyard to get beads. He was trying to cut down on the number of lies he'd been telling lately.

The streamers committee was finally done. So was the napkins-and-cupcakes committee.

The red-hearts committee had only a few more red hearts to put up.

"Doesn't the room look beautiful!" exclaimed Mrs. Morrison. "Let's say thank you to all the children who gave up their recess to make our room look so attractive." There was a general round of applause. A few boys hooted. "Well, now that that's done, what do you say we get a little social studies in?"

What was taking Fletcher so long? How long could it take to run one block, pick up a bag of beads, and run one block back? Then Gopher remembered that Fletcher had said he'd bring a sandwich instead of going home for lunch. What kind of sandwich was he making?

"Take your seats," Mrs. Morrison directed.

Gopher had to think of something fast. Fletcher was a goner if everyone sat down and his seat was discovered empty. Gopher went up to Mrs. Morrison, who was at her desk.

"Yes, Matthew?"

"Since Mrs. Riley's class is also having a Valentine's Day party and since everybody's all excited anyway, do you think we could go see how their room looks? All decorated and everything, I mean?"

Mrs. Morrison looked at her class of rowdy fifth graders. Only two or three children had taken their seats. "Well, it does seem hopeless to get any work done, doesn't it?" She sounded as if she wasn't really in the mood to settle down to work, either. "You go see if Mrs. Riley would welcome a visit from our class. If she says okay, we'll go for a few minutes."

Gopher went to Mrs. Riley and delivered Mrs. Morrison's message. Mrs. Riley was quick to say yes. Apparently she was having the same problem with her class.

"All right, everybody, line up at the door," announced Mrs. Morrison. "We're going to make a little visit to Mrs. Riley's room. I have a Valentine's Day story I can read. It's kind of cute."

A few boys groaned. "A Valentine's Day story!"

"Don't worry," said Mrs. Morrison with a laugh. "It's not the mushy kind."

Gopher dashed to his desk and got out a piece of yellow paper. Quickly he wrote:

> *Fletcher—*
> *We're in Mrs. Riley's room. No one*
> *knows you're missing. Just wait*
> *around and when we come out, act*
> *like you were here all the time.*
>
> *Gopher*

Gopher folded the note and put Fletcher's name on the outside. As the class was filing out of the room he ran and poked the note over Fletcher's coathook. Fletcher would be sure to see it there. If he did what the note said, he'd probably be safe . . . *if* he got back in time.

"I'll Meet You in the Furnace Room"

Gopher didn't see Fletcher immediately when Mrs. Morrison led her class out of Mrs. Riley's room. But by the time the class was filing back into their own room, Fletcher was among the group, near the back.

"Thanks for the note," he whispered.

"It's okay. Did you get the stuff?"

"I sure did."

"Okay, I'll meet you in the furnace room right when the lunch bell rings. Did you bring your lunch?"

"Yeah, I grabbed some cookies."

Gopher gave Fletcher a look. "I thought you took so long because you were making your lunch. What *were* you doing?"

"I was getting the stuff, I told you."

"Okay, okay. See you when the bell rings."

When the lunch bell rang, Stephanie came up to Gopher. "I hope the word *eggplant* doesn't need to be mentioned again today," she teased.

"No, I remembered my money today," he said. "By some miracle."

"Does it take a miracle to remember twenty cents?" she asked, still rubbing it in.

If she only knew, thought Gopher. Maybe someday, a long time from now, he'd tell her. "Anyway, I'm not going to the lunchroom today," he said. "I'm going to the furnace room to work on the valentine some more."

"Oh, don't worry about what all the kids are saying," she said in a sweet voice. "Your valentine is *fine*." Gopher winced. He knew she meant it in the kindest way, but if there was one thing he didn't want to hear, it was that his valentine was "fine." He wanted it to be "tremendous" or nothing at all.

"By the way," he said, hoping to change the subject, "that twenty cents you let me keep yesterday really came in handy. The bill came to two ninety-nine, and I had forgotten the tax! I thought I was a goner and then, wow, there was your money right in my pocket."

"What are friends for?" Stephanie flashed him that beautiful metallic-toothed smile. "See you at the party."

Gopher found his lunch bag and walked to the furnace room. Fletcher was already there, hunched over a pile of colorful beads spread out on the warm cement floor. The red-faced fat lady, with her doily fans and bunched-up bow, lay there, too. "How do you want to do this?" Fletcher asked, not looking up.

Gopher squatted next to Fletcher. "Boy, these are really neat!" He picked up a purple bead and looked at it closely. "This one seems to have dirt stuck to it." He rubbed at some gray caked-on material with his thumbnail.

"That's not dirt," said Fletcher. "That's clay from the Christmas tree. The reason I took so long was that I found I didn't have as many beads left over as I thought. I had to dig a lot of these out of the Christmas tree."

"You mean," Gopher gasped, finding it hard to believe, *"you ruined the Christmas tree?"* He struggled to find the right words. "It was so . . . so . . . " With its bones and fur, it wasn't really "beautiful," and yet it was.

Fletcher shrugged. "It wasn't doing anybody any good. Just collecting dust. Besides, I *said* I was going to bring some beads, didn't I?"

At that moment Gopher really *liked* Fletcher. The guy was acting like a real friend. Because he'd *said* he would bring some beads, he'd ruined his—beautiful—Christmas tree! Gopher waited for Fletcher to look up. When he did, if only for a second, Gopher said, simply, "Thanks."

Fletcher shrugged again and turned his full attention to the valentine. "If I were you," he said, "I'd make little bunches of beads at the base of every doily thingamajig. That would look like jewels, you know, the way they put them in kings' and queens' crowns. It would also cover up the staples you used to attach the doilies."

Gopher had been planning to sprinkle the beads here and there, as he had with the candy hearts. He immediately saw that Fletcher's idea was much more artistic.

"And instead of having the ribbon in a big bunch, we could take it off and weave it in and out around the gold heart in the center. That would look better."

Gopher agreed to both of Fletcher's suggestions, and the two boys got to work. Fletcher glued beads. Gopher worked with the ribbon.

"I sure hope this dries in time," said Gopher. "Wouldn't it be funny if everything fell off in Mrs. Morrison's lap just as we give it to her?" Fletcher laughed a small laugh at Gopher's attempt at a joke.

With the last beads in place and the ribbon finally attached, the valentine was finished. There was an embarrassed silence. Now what should they do? Gopher remembered lunch. "You wanna eat?" he asked.

"Sure," said Fletcher. He pulled a plastic bag out of his pocket. It was half full of store-bought chocolate chip cookies. "Want some?" he offered.

"Okay." Gopher grabbed two slightly crushed cookies. "Want half a baloney sandwich?" Fletcher accepted it. The two boys ate for a few minutes in silence.

The first bell rang. That meant there were five more minutes to get to class. Gopher gently pulled at one of the beads to see if the glue was dry. It wasn't completely, but it was good enough.

"Okay, let's go." He picked up the valentine. Then he stopped and put it down again. "Fletcher! You're the only kid in the class who didn't sign this thing. Quick, write your name." He handed Fletcher a Q-tip and the small jar of gold paint.

Fletcher suddenly became very interested in fiddling with a small piece of glue stuck to his hand. "What's the matter?" asked Gopher in an irritated tone. "You *still* don't want to sign?"

A Few More Changes

Fletcher scanned every detail of the furnace room floor before responding. "It's not because I don't *want* to sign," he finally mumbled. "I don't think I *should* sign." He picked at the glue some more. "All the kids know I didn't pay a quarter. They'll think I'm sponging."

"That's plain stupid!" Gopher was so relieved to learn the real reason Fletcher wasn't signing that he blurted out the words without thinking. "You donated all the beads. They're worth a lot more than a quarter."

Fletcher didn't look convinced.

By this time Gopher really *wanted* Fletcher to sign. He thought of another argument. "And since when do you care what kids think, anyway? You're the only kid I know who goes around bragging that his own brother's in jail."

Fletcher winced. It was clear he didn't take it as the joke Gopher had intended. Having a brother in jail, even if you were proud of it, wasn't funny, Gopher decided.

Fletcher fiddled some more with the glue. "I just made that up," he mumbled, even more softly than before. "I don't have a brother in jail. He's in college."

"He's in college!" Gopher thought about that afternoon he had waited under the big tree, how he had been so terrified that Fletcher was coming back with a knife. "So he never stabbed anybody?" he asked.

"Nah, he doesn't do stuff like that. He's a pretty good guy, actually. He helped me a lot with the television."

Gopher was having trouble getting this to sink in. "Then why did you say such terrible things about him?" he asked. "If I had a brother, I'd never say anything like that."

Fletcher scowled. "What do you mean, *if* you had a brother?"

Now it was Gopher's turn to be embarrassed. "I guess I kind of made that up, too."

"I'd say we're doing pretty good this lunch hour," said Fletcher. With a hint of a laugh he started counting off on his fingers. "We finished the valentine, had lunch, got my brother out of jail and into college, and zapped your 'brother' into . . . " He gestured to show he didn't know where brothers who had never existed went once they were zapped.

"Yeah," Gopher agreed. Fletcher seemed to have a sense of humor. That was another thing Gopher had never known.

"But why *did* you say your brother was in jail?" he asked again. "I made up having a brother because I was scared of you. You weren't scared of anybody."

Fletcher resumed picking at his hand and finally dislodged a pesky piece of glue and flicked it away. "I thought maybe the kids would sort of think it was . . . you know, that I was kind of a tough guy, and then they might sort of . . . well, let me hang around with them."

Gopher couldn't help but snicker. "You sure went about it in a funny way."

Fletcher gave a self-conscious smile. "I'm not going to keep it up. It was a dumb idea to begin with."

"It sure was," Gopher agreed.

"But you're still going to help me carry the television set, aren't you?" Fletcher sounded worried.

Gopher looked him steadily in the eye. "I *said* I would, didn't I?"

Fletcher answered with a grin.

The second bell rang. Everyone was supposed to be in class.

"Fletcher, we've got to go!" Gopher wailed. "Will you *please* sign the stupid valentine? I'll see to it that everybody knows you're not a sponger." He opened the jar of gold paint and handed Fletcher a Q-tip.

"Well, if that's the way you want it . . . "

Fletcher dipped the swab into the paint and quickly wrote his name in an empty space near the bottom.

Gopher blew on the paint to dry it more quickly. Holding the valentine at arm's length, he took another good look. With the beads and ribbon, he decided, the valentine was pretty close to "tremendous" after all. "Looks good," he said simply.

Fletcher nodded he thought so, too.

"But now we really have to go!"

The Party

When they got to the classroom, everybody was already in their seats and Mrs. Morrison was explaining something at the front of the class. The two boys listened outside the door. "So, to make your own valentine folder, you may start with this red construction paper and then decorate it with these ribbons and doilies and such that I picked up at the store. I apologize for not having a better selection—you wouldn't believe how much all these materials cost."

"Do we hafta?" asked a voice. Gopher couldn't see who it was, but it sounded like Lance.

"No, you don't 'hafta,' " said Mrs. Morrison.

"But how are you going to get your valentines home without dropping them?"

"In fourth grade we just took them home in a paper bag," said the same voice, almost certainly Lance's.

"Okay, you may use a paper bag," said Mrs. Morrison.

"I don't have one," said Lance.

Gopher, still outside the door, whispered to Fletcher, "Oh, no, I forgot to bring in valentines! I got too involved with this." He pointed to the red-faced fat lady. Now that he wasn't so embarrassed by the way it turned out, he didn't mind thinking of it as that.

"Well, at least you have an excuse," said Fletcher. "I didn't bring any valentines either."

Gopher grinned. He and Fletcher had something else in common. "Let's just say the dog ate 'em," he joked.

They put the class valentine right outside the door, so it would be handy when the time came, and walked into the classroom. Everybody except Lance was busy with scissors and paste, putting together red valentine folders. It was a project very similar to Gopher's the night before. He enjoyed hearing complaints from various parts of the room about how bad they were turning out. Yeah, well, now they knew.

Gopher considered making a valentine folder, too, since he probably would receive some valentines. But then he thought about Fletcher. Fletcher was standing by himself, just kind of watching what everybody was doing. He wasn't going to make a folder, and Gopher knew why. Fletcher probably thought he wouldn't get many valentines, maybe none. Gopher decided not to make a folder, either.

"Okay, class, are we almost ready for the party?" asked Mrs. Morrison after half an hour or so. "Please line up your folders along the blackboard and we'll all distribute our valentines in a few minutes. In the meantime, let's clean up."

As all the kids started doing what Mrs. Morrison said, Brenda came up to Gopher.

"Okay, when Mrs. Morrison says to start handing out the valentines, I say, 'Wait a minute,'
and you say, 'This valentine is from the whole
class,' and give it to her. But let me see it first,
just to make sure it's okay."

"C'mon, Fletcher," said Gopher, "let's
show her."

Brenda looked confused, as if she was saying, "You're asking *him* to come along?"

"Yeah," said Gopher, answering her look.
"This is Fletcher's valentine, too."

"It is?"

Brenda crossed her arms and tapped her foot
as she studied the valentine. "Not bad," she
said. "I like it."

Gopher nudged Fletcher in the ribs. "She
likes it," he said, wiggling his eyebrows.

When they walked back in, Mrs. Morrison
was speaking very seriously. " . . . and please,
no counting your valentines and comparing
how many you got and how many your neigh-
bor got. And if you didn't bring valentines for
whatever reason, don't feel bad. The spirit of

the holiday is love. All that counting and comparing kind of goes against that, wouldn't you say?"

"*Stand up,*" hissed Brenda to Gopher. "Mrs. Morrison," she called without raising her hand.

"Yes, Brenda?"

"The whole class chipped in and we had Gopher make you something. We'd like to give it to you now, if it's okay."

"Certainly, it's okay," said Mrs. Morrison. "And thank you very much."

Gopher took the valentine from beside his desk and stood up. "Well, actually, Fletcher and I made it together. So I'd like him to come give it with me."

He motioned to Fletcher to walk with him to the front of the class.

"Me?" asked Fletcher. He didn't seem to want to go, but with a little more urging, he got up and walked to the front.

"Well, that's absolutely *beautiful!*" said Mrs. Morrison. She seemed to really like the red-faced, etc. "Thank you so much, Gopher." She

hugged him, not a close hug but a teacher-type hug. Then she realized that Fletcher was standing there, too, and she did the same thing to him.

She looked at the valentine some more. "I love it! And you all signed your names!" She frowned at the class, pretending to be annoyed. "So *that's* why you all had to go to the bathroom so many times this morning."

Everybody laughed, and Mrs. Morrison said she was going to take the valentine home and display it in her living room.

Then it was time to pass out the individual valentines and drink lemonade (pink, for the occasion) and eat cupcakes and candy. Since neither Fletcher nor Gopher had valentines to pass out, they just kind of stood together and watched and ate.

While they were standing there, Stephanie came up to them. "Hey, you guys," she said. "I have valentines for each of you, but you didn't make folders for me to put them in. I think I'll put them right here." With that she proceeded to tape a small valentine onto each of their foreheads.

Gopher looked at Fletcher and Fletcher looked back. Gopher naturally couldn't tell what his own valentine said, but Fletcher's was a picture of a beehive with the words *Bee my friend* on it. If Gopher looked as ridiculous as Fletcher did with that valentine stuck on his forehead, he must have looked pretty silly.

But, he decided, he didn't really care.

About the Author

Virginia Scribner works as a librarian at an elementary school in Rhode Island. She wrote *Gopher Takes Heart* while on sabbatical in California.

Ms. Scribner says she likes to write about fifth graders because third, fourth, and fifth graders "care so much." She hopes children will recognize themselves in her characters.

The idea of *Gopher Takes Heart* came from real life. For several weeks a bully used to stop her son's bicycle, hold the front tire between his legs, and say, "Gimme a quarter!" It was believed that his older brother, like Fletcher's in the story, was also in jail. From there Ms. Scribner made up the rest of the story, trying to make it as real as possible. (She says the only part that's unrealistic is where Mrs. Kelly, a school librarian like herself, puts a filmstrip away in the wrong drawer.)

Ms. Scribner lives in Peace Dale, Rhode Island, with her husband, Elie. They have three grown-up children.